P9-CQW-656

THE MYSTERY BOOKSTORE

created by
GERTRUDE CHANDLER WARNER

Illustrated by Charles Tang

SCHOLASTIC INC.
New York Toronto London Auckland Sydney

ISBN 0-590-20293-6

Copyright © 1995 by Albert Whitman & Company. All rights reserved. Published by Scholastic Inc., 555 Broadway, New York, NY 10012, by arrangement with Albert Whitman & Company. THE BOXCAR CHILDREN is a registered trademark of Albert Whitman & Company.

12 11 10 9 8 7 6 5 4 3 2 1   5 6 7 8 9/9 0/0

Printed in the U.S.A.   40

First Scholastic printing, September 1995

Contents

CHAPTER 1

Going, Going, Gone!

"Next to be auctioned is this toy boxcar," a man yelled to the crowd in the courtyard. "A fine thing for a fine boy or girl. Do I hear a dollar?"

Benny Alden wriggled in his seat. He was so excited he could hardly sit still. He reached into the pocket of his jeans. The seven dollars from the paper route the six-year-old shared with his brother and two sisters was still there, safe and sound.

Benny tugged at his sister's sleeve. "Should I put my hand up now, Jessie?"

"Not yet," twelve-year-old Jessie Alden whispered back, calm as could be. "We don't want to raise the price too soon."

Benny sputtered like an old teakettle. "But . . . Jessie! It looks almost like the boxcar we used to live in."

Jessie pushed back the hair from Benny's forehead. "Don't worry, Benny. Let's just wait a little bit longer."

A couple of voices in the audience called out bids.

"I hear a dollar. Now I hear two dollars," the auction man shouted. "Do I hear three?"

"Three!" Benny yelled before Jessie could stop him.

"I hear three from the boy in the second row," the man said. "Do I hear four dollars?" the man asked.

Everyone in the courtyard was silent. The four Alden children tried hard not to show how much they wanted the old tin boxcar.

"Going once, going twice, going to the boy in the second row!" The man brought down the auction hammer with a bang.

"Yippee!" Benny cried. "We got the box-car!"

"That ends the first half of our auction," the auctioneer announced. "We'll return in fifteen minutes to the main portion of the sale. That's when the Old Treasures Book-shop goes on the auction block. Meanwhile, enjoy the break, folks. You'll find some of our famous New Orleans specialties at the food table in back."

The Aldens, along with their grandfather and his old friend Olivia Chase, got up to stretch their legs. They walked to the back of a courtyard just behind a dusty old bookshop.

Miss Chase smiled at the Aldens a bit nervously. "Thank you for bringing your family to the auction, James. Buying the bookshop is such a big decision. Perhaps you, Henry, Jessie, Violet — and of course Benny here — can bring me good luck."

"Just don't yell out anything too fast," Benny advised the older woman. "Jessie said that just makes the price go up."

Jessie tossed back her long brown ponytail

and looked up at Miss Chase. "Grandfather taught us to be patient at an auction and not jump in too soon."

"Like I just did!" Benny said with a big laugh. "But I had to have this little boxcar for my train collection. It looks almost like the one we lived in before Grandfather found us."

"Except it doesn't have shelves inside or straw beds or a nice tree stump in front of it," Violet said. "Or a cracked pink cup, either." Like her brothers and sister, ten-year-old Violet just loved talking about the old boxcar days when they'd lived in the woods all on their own after their parents died.

"I certainly do love hearing about your boxcar adventures," Miss Chase said. "The story of how your grandfather found you is better than any mystery I could ever write."

"Almost as good as *The Streetcar Mystery*," fourteen-year-old Henry said. "That's my favorite Olivia Chase mystery."

"Every one of your mysteries is a good

read, Olivia," Mr. Alden told his old friend. "I always feel as if I'm right here in New Orleans every time I read one."

"Me, too," Jessie agreed. "Except for Grandfather, this is our first time in New Orleans. But we already feel right at home from reading your books."

Miss Chase blushed at all the attention. "Why, thank you, Jessie. I know my new bookshop will be a big success if there are enough mystery lovers like you Aldens." Suddenly Olivia Chase got a faraway look. "I just hope the bidding doesn't go too high, that's all."

"It's a shame the owner, Mrs. Post, died before she could sell the bookshop to you directly, Olivia," Mr. Alden said. "I know she enjoyed the idea of the Old Treasures Bookshop becoming the Mystery Bookstore."

"It's very difficult to think I might not get the shop," Miss Chase said in a sad voice.

Violet tried to help Miss Chase feel better. "Don't worry. We'll help you follow the bidding so you don't miss out. Grandfather taught us how to watch people's faces when they're bidding."

Miss Chase patted Violet's hand. "I hope no one watches *my* face too closely, or they'll know how much I want it. I've dreamed of opening a mystery bookshop in New Orleans ever since I decided to take a break from writing."

"Has anyone noticed that man?" Henry asked suddenly. "He's been right behind us all this time."

Miss Chase turned to see who Henry was talking about. She saw a middle-aged man with jet black hair quickly move away when he saw that the Aldens were staring at him. Miss Chase fanned herself with the auction booklet. "Oh dear, I'm so nervous, I didn't even notice that Rexford Phillips was right behind us. And me, a mystery writer, too! I should be listening and watching other bidders, not the other way around."

"Is that the fellow you told me was always bothering Mabel Post?" James Alden asked his old friend.

"He's the one," Miss Chase whispered.

"Rex pestered poor Mrs. Post for months about selling the shop to him. He wanted to open a stamp shop here. We both went to the estate lawyers about buying the shop after Mabel's death. That's when they decided to hold an auction. He already bought Mrs. Post's stamp albums. Now I guess he'll be bidding against me for the shop, too."

"What if I sit next to him in case he writes down his bid?" Benny asked after Mr. Phillips left. "I could cough or wriggle my nose or do something to let you know what he wrote down."

"You rascal!" Jessie said, patting Benny on the back. "I guess I've been reading you too many of Miss Chase's mysteries."

Everyone stopped talking when they heard a bell. The second part of the auction was about to start.

"This is your chance, Olivia," Mr. Alden said. "Now go sit in the front with my grandchildren, and I'll keep an eye on everything from back here. Good luck."

Miss Chase and the Alden children seated themselves in the middle row, not too close and not too far from the front.

The auctioneer began with a little talk about the Old Treasures Bookshop. ". . . And included with the shop are all its books as well. The estate lawyers just made a last-minute decision to sell Mrs. Post's books with the building rather than auction them off separately. Sorry about the change in plans, folks."

This news upset Miss Chase and several others in the audience. "Oh, no," she said to the Aldens. "I wasn't planning on buying the books, too. I won't be able to afford them *and* the shop. Not to mention all the work that will involve. Oh dear."

The auction man went on. "Those of you who knew Mrs. Post know that she hid a lot of treasures in her store. This is a very fine New Orleans property smack in the middle of our historic French Quarter. And who knows what all these books might be worth? We'll start the bidding at fifty thousand dollars. That's rock bottom."

Now it was Miss Chase who could hardly sit still. Her foot was tapping, and she kept her hands folded on her lap to keep from calling out a bid too early.

"Sixty-thousand dollars," someone bid.

The audience gasped. A ten-thousand-dollar jump!

"I have sixty thousand, do I hear sixty-five thousand?" the auctioneer said.

"Sixty-five thousand," a voice called out.

Henry turned his head ever so slightly in the direction of this voice.

"It's that Mr. Phillips," Henry whispered to Miss Chase. "He just entered the bidding."

"Maybe it's time for me to bid something, too, but the price is already so high," Miss Chase said.

Before Miss Chase put up her hand, another voice raised the bid. "Sixty-six thousand," an elderly man in the front row shouted.

"Oh my," Miss Chase said to Henry. "That's Ezra Bindry. I didn't know he was back in New Orleans. He's a rare book collector. He knew Mrs. Post quite well."

"Seventy thousand," Rex Phillips called

out even before the auctioneer could get a word in.

"Do I hear seventy thousand, five hundred?" the auctioneer asked the bidders.

Once again, the Aldens saw Mr. Bindry start to raise his hand.

Miss Chase could sit still no longer. "Seventy thousand . . . five hundred," she said in a nervous voice.

Benny gave Miss Chase the thumbs-up sign.

"Seventy-five thousand dollars!" Mr. Bindry yelled.

Up ahead, Mr. Phillips jumped up from his seat. He turned and stared first at Miss Chase then at Mr. Bindry. Finally, Mr. Phillips shouted: "I bid eighty thousand dollars."

There was a hush in the audience. Over the thumping sounds of their hearts, the Aldens heard the screech of a metal chair. Mr. Bindry got up from his seat and stomped out of the courtyard.

Jessie leaned over to Miss Chase. "That's one less bidder anyway."

Miss Chase shook her head sadly. "It

doesn't matter. I can't go any higher, either. Mr. Bindry has lost the shop, and so have I."

Even the auctioneer seemed surprised that in such a short time the Old Treasures Bookshop had gone from fifty thousand to eighty thousand dollars with so few bidders. He paused before moving on. "I've got eighty thousand dollars for this fine old landmark and its contents," he said slowly. "Do I hear more?"

"More," Benny whispered under his breath.

"Shh," Jessie warned. "You don't want to buy a bookstore by accident, now do you?"

"Sorry, Jessie," Benny whispered back. "I got my boxcar, and now I want Miss Chase to get her store, that's all."

"I've got a final bid of eighty thousand dollars. Going once," the auctioneer said, raising his gavel. "Going twice . . ."

"One hundred thousand dollars," a new bidder called out in a deep voice. "I bid one hundred thousand dollars."

Everyone in the audience turned in the direction of the man's voice. Who was this new bidder?

CHAPTER 2

A Surprise Bidder

"Grandfather!" the children said, laughing and hugging Mr. Alden when the auction was over. "*You* bought the bookshop!"

Everyone seemed amazed except for Benny. "Now we have a toy boxcar, a real boxcar, *and* a bookstore. What a good idea!"

"But what will we do with a bookstore, Grandfather?" Jessie asked in her practical way. "Greenfield is so far away from New Orleans, and you're leaving on business tomorrow for a week."

Trying to hide a smile, Mr. Alden scratched his chin. "Hmm. If only we knew someone who knows all about books . . . someone who has always wanted to run a bookstore."

Violet slipped her hand into her grandfather's. "You bought it for Miss Chase, didn't you, Grandfather?" Violet whispered.

Miss Chase was still sitting in her seat, looking awfully confused.

"No, Violet," Mr. Alden said, shaking his head. "I didn't buy it for Miss Chase. I bought it as an excellent investment at a good price. I expect to rent it to whomever can get a bookstore up and running right away." Mr. Alden smiled at his old friend. "Now you wouldn't happen to know anyone who can do that, would you, Olivia?"

"Oh, James, I couldn't possibly let you give the shop to me. You won it fair and square," Miss Chase said.

"Ah, but I wouldn't be giving it to you, I'd be renting it to you until you can pay me back. And who knows? The bookshop was called Old Treasures. You might find something valuable tucked away. What do you say to my plan, Olivia?"

Miss Chase broke into a beautiful smile. "I'll say yes, but only if you lend me your grandchildren, too. With their help we'll sell all these old books at a big outdoor sale. That will give us money to buy brand-new mysteries for my mystery bookstore."

"Can we, Grandfather?" Benny asked excitedly. "Can we stay and help Miss Chase?"

"Of course," Grandfather said. "As long as Olivia doesn't mind looking after four children."

"Hooray!" the Alden children yelled.

Suddenly, a young woman with curly reddish hair rushed into the courtyard.

"Is this where the book auction is?" the woman asked, out of breath. "Has it started yet?"

Rex Phillips stepped forward to answer the young woman's question. "Start?" he said in a snarling voice. "The auction started and ended quickly when someone bid too much for this rundown old property and all the junk inside it!" With that, Mr. Phillips left.

The young woman raced over to the auctioneer. "Please," she said. "Let me put in a bid for some of the books in the shop. My plane was late, and the taxi driver got lost. That's why I didn't get here on time. If you'll only tell me what the other bidders paid for the books, I'll pay more."

The auctioneer pointed to Mr. Alden. "All the books were sold with the shop, Miss. The new owner's over there. You'll have to speak to him about buying any of the books inside the shop. Once my hammer comes down on the last bid, my job is over."

The young woman wouldn't give up. "*Everything* was sold?"

The auctioneer packed up his papers. "Everything. I'm sorry, but you'll have to take matters up with Mr. Alden."

The woman pushed her way past the auctioneer and walked straight toward James Alden. "Mr. Alden, Mr. Alden. May I speak with you? I'm Sarah Deckle. I heard you're running this shop now. I must discuss something with you. You see, I'd like to buy some of the books from you. The only reason I didn't bid at the auction was that my plane was. . . ."

"Whoa, Miss Deckle," Mr. Alden said to calm down the woman. "First off, I'm not running the shop. In fact, I'm only visiting New Orleans. I have to leave tomorrow morning. My good friend over here, Olivia Chase, is in charge now. She's going to turn the Old Treasures Bookshop into the Mystery Bookstore. So anything you need to discuss, well, you'll have to talk to her."

Sarah Deckle grabbed Olivia Chase's arm. "Can I meet with you to talk about the store? It's not fair that I didn't get here in time to bid at the auction. Is there any way I can take a look inside?"

Miss Chase took a while to answer. "Of course, young lady. We're planning to hold a big book sale this weekend and will open the Mystery Bookstore shortly afterwards. You're more than welcome to come."

"But you don't understand," Sarah interrupted. "I need to look . . . I mean, couldn't

I just look through the shop right now? I have money with me."

Olivia shook her head. "I'm sorry, my dear. There are several things we must do before I let any customers look over anything. First of all, I have to get a rare-book expert to come in. There may be something of value in the old books and papers Mrs. Post left behind. I can't let any customers in just yet. You understand, don't you?"

Sarah Deckle did not understand at all. Looking quite upset, she left the courtyard without another word.

"My goodness," Miss Chase said. "What was that all about? Well, never mind. We have lots to do, including getting you children settled in my apartment. I have a special surprise for you."

After everyone left the courtyard with their auction items, Miss Chase locked the gate. "This will be your own private little backyard." Then she pointed up to a beautiful screened-in balcony above the bookstore. "That's a sleeping porch with four cots — one for each of you. On hot nights, we Southerners sometimes like to sleep out on our porches. You'll be perfectly safe, since the courtyard is always locked when the bookshop is closed."

Miss Chase led the children up ironwork stairs to the porch.

"Yippee," Benny said. "We like sleeping outside."

"I knew this would be just right for you," Miss Chase said with a laugh. "Your grandfather will be in the guest room."

"I like your cozy apartment," Violet said as Miss Chase gave the children a tour. "The front of it is like a city apartment where we can watch all the people and cars. But the back is just as quiet as Grandfather's house in Greenfield."

"I was very lucky to rent this apartment from Mrs. Post when I came to New Orleans a few years ago," Miss Chase said, as she handed sheets and towels to the Aldens. "To live above a bookstore is perfect for a writer. Now I can always keep an eye on the Mystery Bookstore, too."

"There's even a small night table for each of us," Violet said, putting down her backpack and tote bag. "Thank you for letting us stay out here."

"You're welcome, Violet," Miss Chase said. "Now, it's been a long day. Good night."

"Don't let the bedbugs bite," Benny said.

The next morning, the Aldens sat around the breakfast table making their plans for the day. From the kitchen in Olivia Chase's apartment, they could look down at the courtyard. But the children were busy chatting and eating, not looking outside.

"These are the best doughnuts I ever tasted," Benny said between bites of warm, powdered doughnuts.

"Those aren't just ordinary doughnuts, Benny," Miss Chase said. "They're a special New Orleans kind called *beignets*. I picked them up at the French Market this morning. As for your coffee, James, that's our New Orleans-style coffee. It has chicory in it."

"Grandfather's coffee has chickens in it?" Benny cried.

Everyone was laughing so hard, they didn't hear the courtyard door open down below.

"Not chickens, Benny." Miss Chase laughed. "It's *chicory*, a special coffee flavoring."

It was only later, when Benny and Henry were washing dishes, that Benny saw something move. "Is the bookshop open?" he asked Miss Chase. "I think somebody wearing a blue top is down in the courtyard."

But when Benny and the other children ran to the sleeping porch to check, the person in the blue top had vanished.

"Hey, where did that person go?" Benny yelled. "Nobody went out that door."

"Are you sure you saw someone?" Miss Chase asked Benny. "I'm sure I locked the courtyard door. Remember? Maybe what you saw was one of those boxes blowing around from the auction yesterday."

"But boxes don't wear blue tops," Benny

said. "We better go check it out."

"Good for you, Benny," Miss Chase said. "A careful detective follows every lead. You children can go downstairs. Let me know if anything seems disturbed. I'll be right down. I'm just going to call in an ad to the newspaper. I need a book expert to help us price Mrs. Post's old books for our book sale."

"Then I'll be off too, Olivia," Mr. Alden said. "My taxi will be here any second. I'll be back in a week."

The children hugged their grandfather, then raced down to the courtyard. They had just reached the bottom step when they heard the courtyard door click shut.

"See!" Benny cried. "Somebody *was* here. They must have left when they heard us." He pulled at the door, but it wouldn't open.

"I guess it locks from both sides," Henry said. "I'll get Miss Chase's key."

When Henry returned, he unlocked the courtyard door. Benny raced out to the sidewalk. "See, there's someone with a blue shirt going down the block! I told you."

Violet put her arm around Benny, then

pointed to another person on the busy street. "And there's someone else with a blue top."

"There's that woman who came late to the auction," Jessie said. She pointed to Sarah Deckle, who was staring into the bookstore window. "She has on a blue jacket."

"Even Grandfather is wearing blue today," Henry said to a disappointed Benny. "Look, he's getting in his taxi to go to the airport. He has on his blue blazer."

"Even I'm wearing a blue shirt," Benny said. "Today must be Wear-Something-Blue Day." Then Benny had to laugh.

The Aldens walked back into the courtyard to begin cleaning up. There was plenty to do before the big book sale.

"Any luck with the mystery person?" Miss Chase asked when she came down to see how the Aldens were getting on.

"No," Benny answered, "but somebody was here all right. And they left in a big, big hurry when they heard us."

Miss Chase stopped to look at something under the sleeping porch. "I think Benny's right. Come here and tell me what you see."

The Aldens stared down at the patch of dirt and weeds under the porch.

"Look! There are clumps of dirt from here to the courtyard door," Violet said. "And some of the weeds are squished. But couldn't that be from yesterday? There were a lot of people walking around the courtyard during the auction. Maybe some of them tracked the dirt out."

"Good detective work, Violet," Miss Chase said. "But think some more."

Violet's blue eyes lit up. "Wait! It rained a little bit this morning. If somebody walked through the dirt yesterday, the clumps would have washed away!"

"Very good," Miss Chase said.

"Shh," Benny whispered when a few people wandered into the courtyard to look around. "There's that lady again."

"Why, hello, Miss Deckle," Olivia Chase said to the young woman. "What brings you here so early?"

"I still can't get over missing out on the auction yesterday," Sarah Deckle told Miss Chase. "I would just love to look through your bookshop. Couldn't I take a peek now, please?"

Miss Chase finally gave in. "I guess you can look around. But I can't sell a thing until our book sale on Saturday."

"Thank you! Thank you!" Sarah Deckle said. As soon as Miss Chase opened the bookstore door, the young woman disappeared inside the store without another word.

CHAPTER 3

Violet Gets a Present

The hours flew by. Miss Chase spent her time making business calls. The Aldens carried books from the shop out to the tables in the courtyard where the book sale would be held. And Sarah Deckle spent the morning buried in the children's book section where she seemed to be reading every book from cover to cover.

"This is practically the hardest job I've ever done," Jessie said.

"Harder than cleaning up a boxcar or

working in a pizza restaurant?" Henry asked in amazement.

"These books are just so tempting," Jessie said. "I keep wanting to stop work so I can read them. I wish we were living in the bookshop instead of above it."

"Me, too," Violet confessed. "Here's a neat old book on needlepoint. It's full of patterns I've never seen before." Then Violet showed the others something else she had found. "This beautiful boxed set of fairy tales was mixed in with some stamp collecting books in the hobby box. There are four stories in the set, *Tom Thumb*, *Goose Girl*, *Briar Rose*, and, my favorite of all, *The Little Mermaid*. I'm going to show it to Miss Chase."

Violet found Miss Chase working in the bookstore. "Look at this pretty set of fairy tales, Miss Chase. Should I put it aside? It's got beautiful illustrations."

Miss Chase came over and put her arm around Violet. "The books are lovely. I never noticed them in Mabel Post's shop before, but I guess it's because they were jumbled

up with the hobby books. That Mabel. She liked to just throw everything together! Anyway, you found the set, so I'd like you to keep it, Violet."

Violet shook her head. "No, I couldn't, Miss Chase. What if the set is valuable? You need every penny to buy new books for the Mystery Bookstore." Violet handed the boxed set back to Miss Chase.

"It couldn't be that valuable if Mabel just threw it in with the hobby books. Take it as a thank-you present. You children are saving me many, many more pennies with all your help than this set could possibly be worth," she said.

Violet ran her fingers over the beautiful fairy tale collection. "Thank you. I'll take very good care of them."

Violet and Miss Chase then went back out to the courtyard to see how the work was coming along.

"What else can we do, Miss Chase?" Jessie asked. "We organized all the books out here. We'll put out the children's books after Sarah Deckle leaves."

"I really must get her out of the store," Miss Chase whispered. "She just won't budge."

"I'll go tell her it's lunchtime," Benny suggested. "Because it is!"

Miss Chase laughed. "Good idea, Benny. Nobody would keep a hungry boy from lunch."

But Miss Chase was wrong. When Benny told Sarah Deckle it was lunchtime, the young woman tried to send him away. "Oh, no problem, little boy. Run along. I'll just be a little while longer."

Now Benny Alden liked just about everything, but two things he didn't like were being called a little boy and having to wait for lunch. Those doughnuts seemed an awful long time ago.

"I meant lunchtime for everyone," Benny said in his nicest voice.

Sarah Deckle still didn't move.

"Closing time, closing time!" Miss Chase said in her no-nonsense voice.

"But, but, I'm not finished," Sarah Deckle complained.

"You'll have more than enough time this weekend when the book sale starts," Miss Chase said. "Besides, everything is all dark and musty in here. You can hardly see a thing. By Saturday, we'll have all these books out in the courtyard where it's nice and bright. There, there, Miss Deckle. Now run along and enjoy a good lunch."

"Can we have lunch now, too?" Benny asked.

"We sure can," Miss Chase answered. "Let's go to Mama's Restaurant. It's a couple of blocks away on Magazine Street. It's one of your grandfather's favorite lunch places."

"Then I know it will be mine, too," Benny said.

They were just about to leave when Sarah Deckle turned around one last time.

"I'm going, I'm going," she began, "but I . . . " She stopped talking when she noticed Violet putting the boxed set into Jessie's green backpack so it wouldn't get lost. "May I just look at that set?" she asked.

Miss Chase finally ran out of patience.

"Those books are not for sale, Miss Deckle. For that matter, none of these books are for sale until this weekend. Now these children must have some lunch. I suggest the same for you."

There was no mistaking Olivia Chase this time. She held the courtyard door open until Sarah Deckle finally walked out.

"Whew! I thought it would be dinnertime before she left," Jessie said as they walked down the street. "I could eat two lunches now."

"I could eat two hundred!" Benny said, skipping ahead of everyone.

They were almost at Mama's Restaurant when Miss Chase remembered something. "Henry, would you do me a big favor? Please run back to the courtyard and see if I left my notepad on one of the tables. I have to stop at the office supply store, but I can't remember what was on my list. Here's the key to the courtyard. We'll save a place for you."

"Be back in a flash," Henry said, taking Miss Chase's keys.

When Henry reached the courtyard door he looked down and noticed that the door was opened slightly.

"What?" he said to himself.

Henry pushed the heavy door slowly so it wouldn't squeak. He looked around. Right away he saw that some of the plastic rain sheets on the book tables were folded back.

"Looking for someone?" a man's voice called out.

Henry jumped.

"How did you get in here, Mr. Bindry?" Henry asked the gray-haired man.

"How did you know I was Mr. Bindry?"

"Miss Chase told us at the auction," Henry answered. "She said you were a rare-book expert and that you had known Mrs. Post."

"Olivia should keep her business to herself instead of talking so much to every tourist who passes through," Mr. Bindry said angrily.

"I'm not a tourist," Henry explained. "I mean, I am a tourist, I guess. But I'm here with my brother and two sisters to help Miss Chase get her mystery bookshop ready for business."

"A mystery bookshop!" he shouted. "What nonsense! Olivia should stick to writing books, not selling them."

"How did you get in here?" Henry repeated. "Do you have a key, too?"

"Don't need a key when fool people leave the door wide open," Mr. Bindry said. "I just walked right in."

Henry scratched his head. He was pretty sure they'd locked the door, but he wasn't about to argue with Mr. Bindry. Looking around, Henry spied Miss Chase's notepad lying on one of the tables.

"This is what I came for," Henry explained. "So I guess I'd better lock up. Miss Chase is waiting for me."

Henry waited for Mr. Bindry to leave, but the man didn't seem to want to go. Finally, Henry said, "We're getting all those books ready for a big book sale on Saturday. You can buy anything you want then, Mr. Bindry."

"Hrmph!" was all Mr. Bindry had to say before he was finally good and ready to leave.

Out on the street, Henry double-checked that the courtyard door was really locked this time. He was so busy locking up, he didn't happen to see what Mr. Bindry had tossed in the backseat of his car.

It was a blue jacket.

CHAPTER 4

Snooping Around

"These book tables are as well organized as a library," Miss Chase told the Aldens the next day. "I'm glad to see Violet reading one of her fairy tales because some of these books have been sitting in this shop unread for decades."

Henry laid down an armful of books on a sale table. "We're almost done!" he said. "Now we can clean up the inside of the book-shop before the painters come."

Jessie checked each table to make sure the books were in alphabetical order. She turned to Miss Chase. "I hope you make lots of money on these dusty old books. Then you can order some brand-new ones for your brand-new shop!"

"All that's left is to hire someone who knows a lot about these books to help me price them," Miss Chase said. "I do hope someone will answer my newspaper ad."

"How come you didn't . . ." Jessie started to say before she stopped. She didn't want to be nosy.

". . . hire Ezra Bindry?" Miss Chase said, finishing Jessie's question. "I'd like nothing better. But Ezra goes out of his way to say he doesn't like mystery books — or the people who write them! He's a strange one. He doesn't really read the words in books. He just looks at how they're made, not what they say. They could be shoes or hats or loaves of bread."

"I wish some of these books *were* loaves of bread," Benny said when he heard this.

"What if Mr. Bindry answers your ad?" Violet asked Miss Chase.

"Why, I guess I'd give him the job," Miss

Chase answered. "Maybe now that Mrs. Post docsn't stand between us, I can start fresh with Ezra."

Everyone was surprised to hear someone trying to open the courtyard door.

"That's funny," Violet said when she went to see who was there. "I put a sign up saying we're closed until Saturday." But before she could unlock the door, Violet felt it push open.

"Why, Rex!" Miss Chase said when she saw who was there. "What brings you here?"

Mr. Phillips's answer was a frown. He shifted from foot to foot and dropped his keys. Violet put down her copy of *Tom Thumb* to pick them up.

"I've got them," Mr. Phillips snapped, stepping on his keys. He picked them up and handed Violet her book. "Where'd you get this book anyway?"

"It's a present from me, Rex," Miss Chase said. "I'm sorry, but the shop isn't open for business yet."

Mr. Phillips explained his visit. "Since I'm an old friend of Mabel's, too, I wanted to look around before the sale. I expected to be the owner by now, but you seem to have arranged to get the bookstore for yourself."

Miss Chase blushed at Mr. Phillips's rude remark.

"I didn't arrange anything of the kind, Rex. Mr. Alden is renting me the bookstore. I expect to pay him back shortly. I certainly don't have to explain things any further."

"All right. All right," Mr. Phillips said. "I just want a quick look."

Miss Chase stepped between Mr. Phillips and the book tables. "I'm sorry, Rex. The Aldens have put these books in perfect order for my sale. Everything is all set to be priced. Our sale starts Saturday morning at nine sharp. I will see you then."

With that, Miss Chase guided Mr. Phillips out.

"What a difficult man! He was always pestering Mabel Post, too," Miss Chase explained. "The only thing they had in common was stamp collecting. Rex was convinced Mabel had a valuable stamp she had hidden away. In any case, Rex already bought all her albums. What more could he want?"

"I'm sure glad he left," Henry said. "Now we can get started washing down these shelves before the painters get here."

"Good idea," Miss Chase said. "With all of us pitching in, we'll be done in a snap."

They got right to work. Henry started with the top shelves while the younger children washed the bottom ones.

Benny was full of questions. "Are the painters painting the walls black? Can we keep those cobwebs up on the ceiling? Maybe the shop should look like a haunted house!"

Miss Chase laughed. "I don't know about black walls and cobwebs, Benny, but I love Violet's idea to decorate the store windows and walls with black paper footprints. Oh my, there's someone staring in the window."

The children turned around.

"It's Mr. Bindry," Henry said. "I bet he wants to snoop around like he did yesterday. I told him to come back on Saturday."

Miss Chase opened the bookshop door. "Come in, come in, Ezra," she said, giving the grumpy man a big smile. "Can I help you with anything?"

"I'd like to speak with you privately, Olivia," Mr. Bindry said as he gave the Aldens a disapproving look.

"Oh, these are my helpers, Ezra," she explained. "This is Jessie, Violet, and Benny. Henry told me you met yesterday. I've been so busy I must have left the door unlocked."

"Yes, why yes . . . that's right," Mr. Bindry said. "Anyway, I'm here for the job of pricing the books. Nobody knows more about books in these parts than I do. You couldn't go wrong since I'm already familiar with most of the books from Mabel's shop."

"I'd like that," Miss Chase said.

"Well, these children can't do everything," Mr. Bindry said. "Anyway, children and old books don't mix."

The Aldens looked at each other.

Miss Chase straightened herself. "That's quite enough, Ezra. I'll have you know that the Aldens are completely responsible for getting Mabel's books — I should say my books — in perfect order. Just take a look at those tables out there. There's not a book damaged or out of place."

"Hrmph," Mr. Bindry said, making one of his favorite sounds.

"I simply can't hire you if you're not willing to work with the Aldens," Miss Chase informed the old man. "I plan to repay their grandfather for investing in the shop. I need plenty of help."

Mr. Bindry seemed about to leave but changed his mind. "All right. But just keep these kids out of my hair until Saturday. I'll price the books out in the courtyard. They can work in here."

"I agree you need peace and quiet to do your job," Miss Chase said. "So, here's what we can do. The children need some fun. I'd like them to take a little time off for some sightseeing today and part of each day they're here."

"But we don't need to go sightseeing," Jessie said. "We like helping with your shop just as much. Honest."

Miss Chase smiled. "Now Ezra, how can you resist this lovely family?"

"Hrmph!" Mr. Bindry repeated. He was interested in books, *not* children.

"I guess 'Hrmph' means the arrangement suits you?" Miss Chase asked.

"Hrmph!" Mr. Bindry answered.

"Okay, children," Miss Chase said. "You've done plenty for today. I want you to take a break and go over to the French Market for milk and *beignets*. Before Mr. Bindry gets started, go out to the book tables and choose any books you've had your eyes on. They're yours."

"Choose any books they'd like?" Mr. Bindry shouted, not mumbling at all now. "There might be something here worth hundreds or even thousands of dollars. You can't mean they can choose *any* books?"

Miss Chase folded her arms. "That's exactly what I mean."

Henry picked up some books from the mystery table. "These are by my favorite writer," he said, holding up two mysteries. "Olivia Chase."

"Same here," Jessie said, holding up two other Olivia Chase mysteries.

Benny found an old copy of *The Boy's Handbook*. "Is this worth a lot of money, Mr. Bindry?"

"Hardly!" Mr. Bindry sniffed. "Every boy your age had a copy years ago. They're as common as yesterday's newspaper."

Benny held onto the nice old book all the same.

"What about you, Violet? Don't you want to choose anything?" Miss Chase asked.

"Thank you so much, Miss Chase," Violet said softly. "But I'm happy with my fairy tales."

"Fairy tales? What fairy tales?" Mr. Bindry asked Miss Chase.

Violet held out her copy of *The Little Mermaid*. "Can you tell if this is worth anything? It's part of a boxed set."

Mr. Bindry's eyes widened, and he reached out to examine the book. "Worth something? If it's what I think it is, it's . . ." The old man stopped talking. "It's practically worthless."

Violet bit her lip and hugged the books

tightly. "It's not worthless to me. I'm going to keep the whole set next to my bed so it doesn't get sold by mistake."

"Keep out one book for now, okay, Violet?" Jessie suggested. "That way we'll have something to read if we sit in the park later." Violet nodded and disappeared upstairs to put the rest of the set away.

Miss Chase saw how Mr. Bindry had upset Violet. She guided him to the far end of the courtyard to get him away from the Aldens. "I can't have you talking so sharply to these children, Ezra."

But Mr. Bindry just wouldn't drop the subject. "If you hire someone to fix a car, you don't give the car away before the mechanic opens the hood, Olivia. How can I do my work if you're giving everything away before I even start?"

Miss Chase calmly peeled back the plastic coverings over the book table. "There are plenty of books for you right here, Ezra. I'll get you a notebook and some pencils so you can get started right away."

"Mr. Bindry is so grumpy," Benny told his brother and sisters after they went back inside the bookshop.

"Miss Chase will calm him down," Jessie said."She knows what to do. Now let's put these buckets and sponges away, grab our backpacks, and go to the French Market."

"Do we have to talk French at the French Market?" Benny asked as he finished cleaning up. "All I know is 'French fries.' "

Henry dumped two pails of water into a small sink in the back of the store. "Don't worry," he said.

"I know what I want at the French Market," Benny said. "Those Benny things. . . ."

"*Beignets*," Violet said when she came back downstairs with everyone's backpacks for their outing. "They are yummy."

"Mmm, sounds good to me. Oops," Henry said when they stepped out into the street and he almost tripped. "Here's Miss Chase's newspaper. Let's check for her ad." Henry opened to the classified section. He ran his finger up and down the columns of job ads. "Hmm. It must be in tomorrow's paper."

"Hey, wait a minute!" Jessie cried. "How did Mr. Bindry know about Miss Chase's ad for a book expert if it's not in the paper yet?"

CHAPTER 5

The Face in the Photograph

The Riverfront Streetcar was jammed with people visiting New Orleans just like the Aldens. Everyone seemed to be wearing a silly hat or carrying a colorful souvenir umbrella to shade themselves from the hot sun.

"New Orleans is just like a carnival," Violet said, holding onto the center pole of the streetcar. "They seem to have little parades going on all the time."

"I'm so squished I don't need to hold onto

anything," Benny said. "This streetcar is so crowded."

"Just hang in there, Benny," Henry said. "Miss Chase told us the French Market is only a few stops down the line."

As the streetcar rolled along, the Aldens tried to look at everything at once. Just a few feet from the tracks, the sidewalks were filled with street musicians, food carts, artists painting portraits of tourists, and people buying trinkets from sidewalk stands. The Aldens could hardly wait to join in.

"Jackson Square! Jackson Square!" the conductor called out when the streetcar finally came to a stop.

"Does everyone have everything?" Jessie asked.

The younger children felt for their backpacks. The Aldens liked to carry around whatever they might need on their outings — cameras, books, sketch pads, and snacks in case they got hungry, which they always did.

"Everything's still here but kind of

mashed," Benny said. He looked into his backpack to make sure his cowboy wallet, his new book, and his box of raisins were safe and sound.

"My sketch pad and coin purse are here. But wait, Jessie. Look at your backpack!" Violet cried. "The flap came untied."

Without even checking, Jessie ran alongside the streetcar to see if anything had fallen from her backpack. "Wait!" she called out to the conductor.

But the Riverfront Streetcar had pulled away.

"Too late," Jessie said. She put her pack down on a sidewalk bench. "I'm sure I tied the flap down tight before we left."

Jessie emptied her backpack on the bench. "Let's see if I still have everything. Here's the street map. The Thermos. My address book. My camera and wallet. My mystery book. What else did I have in here? Oh, good, your book is here, too." She picked up *The Little Mermaid* that Violet had stuck in there for reading later on.

With that, Jessie repacked everything and closed the flap. Then she put down her pack on the bench so she could check the map. "Now let's see where we are. According to the map, the French Market and the café Miss Chase told us about should be right in front of us."

"Let's just follow that nice smell," Benny said, sniffing the air.

The other children took a deep whiff, too. A wonderful scent of fried dough, chocolate, and coffee floated around them.

"Mmm, it's coming from over there," Violet said as the children stood on their tiptoes to see over all the people crowding the big square.

"Then let's go," Benny said, pulling on Jessie's arm.

Jessie folded the map and bent down to put it away. "Oh, no," she cried, "my backpack is gone!"

The children looked high and low around the bench and retraced a few steps, but the green backpack was gone.

"Wait. Look at that woman over there," Henry told Jessie. "Isn't that your pack dangling from her arm?"

Jessie didn't take the time to answer. With the other children right behind, she chased after the woman through the crowd, never taking her eyes off the backpack.

When Jessie finally caught up, she tapped the woman's shoulder. "Excuse me," she said, all out of breath.

When the woman turned around, the children all cried at once: "Sarah Deckle!"

Jessie spoke first. "Sarah, is that my backpack you're holding? I left it on a bench so I could read a map. When I turned around, it was gone."

"Why . . . why, yes, I took it. I . . . I mean I saw it lying there on the bench back there. I was going to see if there's a Lost and Found office nearby. Here, take it."

Jessie took the green backpack and slipped her arms into the shoulder straps. "Whew. That was careless of me. Thanks."

Without even a "You're welcome," Sarah Deckle disappeared into the crowd.

"Boy, she didn't seem too happy to give that back to you," Henry said. "I mean, if she was going to the Lost and Found like she said, she should have been pleased you turned up so soon."

"Maybe she wasn't going to the Lost and Found," Violet said. "Maybe she wasn't going to give it back."

"I'm just glad I found it," Jessie said.

"Now can we eat at that good-smelling restaurant over there, Jessie?" Benny asked. "It says 'Café.' I know that means coffee, but I hope they have plain old chocolate milk, too."

"It's called Café du Monde, Benny," Violet said, taking Benny by the hand. "It means 'The People's Café.' "

Benny pulled Violet. "Well, I'm a people, so let's get going!"

The children found a table for four in the open-air café.

"I'll get us some of those *beignet* doughnuts for all of us, while you hold the table," Henry said. "Can I get some money from your wallet, Jessie?"

Jessie took out her camera and handed Henry her backpack.

"I just love New Orleans," Jessie said. "I'm going to try out the new instant camera Grandfather gave me for my birthday."

Jessie stepped back and snapped a picture of Benny making a silly face while Violet giggled at him.

"The photo only takes a couple of minutes to develop," Jessie said. "It's almost ready."

Jessie pulled hard, and a photo slid out of the camera. Everyone watched closely as a picture developed right before their eyes.

"Here I am! Here I am!" Benny said, excited to see himself appear as if by magic in the photo.

Sure enough, there was Benny's silly face and Violet laughing at it.

"Fried *beignets* coming up!" Henry said a few minutes later when he returned with a tray of doughnuts.

Pretty soon the plate of *beignets* in front of the Aldens was a plate of crumbs.

"You'll never guess who was in line with me," Henry said when he had finished eating.

"Sarah Deckle. She was right behind me."

"It's so crowded, I don't see her anywhere, Henry," Violet said. "Do you, Jessie?"

"Me neither," Jessie said, turning her head this way and that. "I guess Sarah Deckle likes these special doughnuts too."

The children left the café and went out to Jackson Square.

"Stand by that big statue of Andrew Jackson on his horse," Jessie said. She arranged Henry and Violet on either side of Benny. Then she stepped back, trying to get everybody in the picture, including the huge bronze horse and its rider.

"Who's Andrew Jackson?" Benny asked Henry as he tried to talk and smile at the same time.

"A war hero from a long time ago during the Battle of New Orleans," Henry said.

"Got it!" Jessie said. She pulled out the instant photo and waited for it to develop.

A few minutes later, the picture was ready. "Oh, no!" Jessie laughed. "Look. I cut off the horse's head and Andrew Jackson in the photo."

"That's okay," Henry said to Jessie. "It takes a while to get used to a new camera. We have lots more places to see in New Orleans, so you'll get plenty of practice with your picture taking."

Ten pictures later, the Aldens collapsed in a little park overlooking the Mississippi River.

"Whew, sightseeing is a lot of work!" Henry said, stretching himself on a patch of green grass along with the other children.

"It sure is," Jessie agreed. "I brought along a small Thermos of lemonade. We'll share it."

The children cooled off with small sips of lemonade while they watched all the riverboats arriving and departing on the river.

Jessie snapped her last picture of the busy scene.

"Can I see? Can I see?" Benny looked over Jessie's shoulder as the instant picture developed.

"Here, I'll spread out all the pictures we took," Jessie said. She arranged the photos in rows on the grass so everyone could get a look.

Henry chuckled as he studied the pictures. "Gosh, Benny. You made a silly face in every single picture, even at that old New Orleans cemetery we visited!"

"I like making faces," Benny said with a laugh. "Hey, there's another face in every picture. But it's not a silly one."

The children leaned in to get a better look.

"It looks like Mr. Phillips!" Violet cried. "He's in the picture Jessie took at the café. Then next to the horse statue. And here in the cemetery. Doesn't that also look like him in this shot of the dock you just took?"

"You're right, Violet," Jessie said. "Let's see if the person is still down there in case it is Mr. Phillips. Some of these pictures are a little blurry."

The children raced down to the riverboat dock. But by the time they got there, the last boat had pulled away, taking with it all the people in Jessie's photo.

CHAPTER 6

The Shadow Knows

"I'm so full, I can hardly walk up these stairs," Benny said as the children climbed up to Miss Chase's apartment. "And guess what? I'm not even hungry! That jumble dish we had for dinner sure filled me up."

"You mean the jambalaya," Violet said.

Jessie stepped into the apartment first. "It's so dark in here. Miss Chase was nice to leave the door unlocked, but I sure wish she had left a light on. I can't see a thing. She must have gone to bed early."

Henry felt around in the dark for a light

switch and flicked it on. "Hey, what's that?" He pointed to a crumpled note lying near the front door and smoothed it out. He read it aloud:

"Dear Aldens,

I hope you've had a wonderful day and evening out in New Orleans. I went out to dinner, too. I have locked the door. I'll be back around ten o'clock. I have my key, so be sure to lock up when you get home.

'Night all,
Olivia Chase."

Henry lowered his voice to a whisper. "We'd better go back out."

"Come along, Violet. You, too, Benny," Jessie whispered.

Thinking about the cozy cot on the sleeping porch, Benny wasn't too happy about turning back. "Why can't we go in?"

"You shouldn't go into a house if the door is unlocked when it shouldn't be. There might be a burglar inside. Miss Chase said she locked the door," Jessie said. She took

Benny by the hand and led him back downstairs and into the courtyard.

"Let's go out to the street and find a phone booth. It can't hurt to call the police to make sure no one is prowling nearby," Henry said. "There's something strange about Miss Chase's apartment being unlocked. Just yesterday, the courtyard was unlocked when it wasn't supposed to be."

Henry unlocked the courtyard gate, and the children stepped onto the sidewalk. Then Benny saw someone step from the shadows of the bookstore doorway.

"Look!" Benny pointed to a figure who darted down the street. "I think that person just came out of the bookstore."

The children ran to the shop doorway. Jessie pulled and pushed the door, but it wouldn't budge. When everyone looked down the street again, the shadow had vanished.

"Benny, are you sure you saw someone come out of the shop?" Jessie asked.

Benny scrunched his forehead. "It was so

dark, I couldn't see. I couldn't even tell if it was a she or a he."

The children heard footsteps on the sidewalk. They belonged to Miss Chase. "Are you just coming home, too?" she said, surprised to see the Aldens. "You must be tired out. Let's get you off to bed after your long day."

"But . . . but," Violet began, "we think there was a prowler in the bookshop or in your apartment. The back door was unlocked, and your note was bunched up on the floor."

"And know what else?" Benny broke in. "A person jumped out of this doorway but then disappeared. Henry was just about to call the police."

Even in the dim street light, the children could see that Miss Chase looked worried. She checked up and down the street and inside the bookshop windows. "You children did just the right thing. Calling the police is a good idea. I'll make the call."

Less than five minutes later, a cruiser arrived in front of the bookshop. Two police officers got out carrying flashlights.

"We got your call, Miss Chase," one of them said. "First, let's check out the shop."

With that, the police examined the bookshop door lock. "Well, it doesn't look forced or anything. Can you unlock it, Miss Chase?"

"Do you see anything missing or disturbed?" one of the police officers asked Miss Chase when they got inside the shop.

"Not that I can tell. You see, we've been unpacking books and cleaning and throwing things out," she explained. "Everybody's been so busy, if someone touched or took anything, it would be hard to tell."

The police led everyone out to the courtyard and flashed their lights up and down the brick walls and book tables. "How about out here? Is everything in order?"

Miss Chase sighed. "Again, it's impossible to say, Officer. Everything looks fine. The children said they found my apartment unlocked. I'm sure I locked it, before I left."

Everyone trooped upstairs to check the apartment. Henry handed the police officer

Miss Chase's crumpled note. "Maybe somebody saw this on the door and somehow got into the apartment when they figured out no one was here."

"We saw a person run from the bookshop doorway when we went out to the front sidewalk," Jessie added. "Maybe the person went up to the apartment, down the stairs into the bookshop, then out the front door to the street."

"Man or woman?" the police officer asked.

"It was too dark to tell," Henry explained. "And the person was halfway down the block by the time we put two and two together. Sorry."

The two officers turned on the lights and led everyone through the apartment. "Just walk through and tell me if you see anything out of place since you left," one of the officers advised.

Miss Chase and the Aldens checked each room. Nothing seemed disturbed in any way. The drawers were all shut. Miss Chase's jewelry box and silverware were neatly in their places. Even Benny's stuffed animal, Stockings, was propped up on the cot on the sleeping porch, exactly where Benny had placed him that morning.

"We'll cruise around the block a few times during the night," one of the officers told Miss Chase, "just in case."

"Good night. Thank you for coming," Miss Chase said.

"No problem," one of the police officers said. "Often kids see things that turn out to be nothing. And everybody forgets to lock their doors once in a while. Why, if I had a dollar for every time somebody called up. . . ."

"Good night, Officer," Miss Chase said, this time a little more firmly.

"The police didn't believe us," Benny said after they had gone. "Just because we're kids."

Miss Chase patted Benny's hand. "Well, I believe you, Benny. I can see the police have made up their minds that I left my apartment unlocked. We'll just have to be extra careful about keeping our eyes and ears open to see if there really is someone snooping around here. We'll be very busy with the book sale and all, but that would be a good time to be on the lookout."

"I learned lots of detective tricks from your books," Jessie said. "We can try them out first thing tomorrow morning."

"How about tonight?" Benny said, suddenly as wide-awake as could be.

"Aren't you tired?" Miss Chase asked, smiling at Benny's liveliness.

"Me, tired?" Benny said. "I'm never tired when there's a mystery to solve. I want to find out if somebody's following us around."

"Well, I'm ready for bed," Miss Chase said. "Good night."

"Where do we start?" Violet asked Henry and Jessie after Miss Chase left.

"Let's check the bookshop again, then the apartment," Henry suggested. "Where are you going, Benny? The stairs to the bookshop are down the hall."

"You'll see," Benny said with a big smile. "Wait for me, okay?"

When Benny came back, he was carrying

a small white-and-pink can of baby powder.

"Where did you get that?" Violet asked.

"From the bathroom. It's for dusting for fingerprints. When Jessie reads me Miss Chase's books, the detective always uses powder to look for fingerprints where the bad guy was."

Henry smiled at Benny. "That works okay in books, but the bookshop will be covered with so many fingerprints from all the customers, we'd have to stay in New Orleans our whole lives before we could check out each print."

"Oh, well," Benny said. "I'll go put it back in the bathroom."

"Wait," Violet said. Then she bent down and whispered something in Benny's ear.

"Goody!" Benny cried, leading the way downstairs.

When Jessie unlocked the inside door of the bookshop, Benny raced over to the front door. He sprinkled powder on the floor. When he was done with that, he sprinkled more powder on the windowsills.

Jessie smiled at Benny. "I bet Violet told

you about how Miss Chase's detective used to put down powder to see if anyone returned to the scene of a crime in *The Streetcar Mystery*. Good work, Benny!"

The children checked the bookshop carefully for any signs of a prowler.

"I can't remember what was over here and what was over there since this morning," Jessie said, after about half an hour of checking the room inch by inch. "We moved everything around so much."

Henry put down one of the books he'd been examining from a box of books in the corner. He yawned. "We ought to call it a night," Henry said, "and start looking again in the morning."

"There's one more thing we can do," Jessie said, handing Benny and Violet some sheets of paper from a notepad. "Tear these in tiny pieces and hide them in different places — inside some of the books that are left and in those boxes of odds and ends."

"I know!" Benny cried. "Those little pieces will fall out if someone picks up stuff with the paper scraps inside. Then we'll

know for sure if somebody touched anything. Neat!"

The Aldens went around hiding the small
paper scraps in as many places as they could.

As soon as they were done, they went upstairs to get ready for bed.

Jessie went over to tuck Benny under his
covers. "Would you like me to read you one
of Violet's fairy tales?"

Benny's answer was a big yawn and lots
of eye rubbing. He hugged Stockings, then
flopped back on his cot. "No stories tonight.
I'm too tired."

CHAPTER 7

A Suspect Turns Up

"Wake up sleepyheads!" Jessie said the next morning. Jessie tickled Violet's and Benny's feet.

"Stop it, Watch," Violet mumbled. Still dreaming, she thought she was back in Greenfield where the family dog, Watch, liked to wake up the children one by one.

Jessie laughed. "It's me, not Watch, silly. No wonder you're both so tired. I heard one of you get up during the night."

Violet finally opened her eyes. She pulled

the covers over her head to keep out the light. "That was Benny who got up."

"Did not," Benny protested.

"Did too," Violet said.

Violet sat up on her cot. "Then I guess you were sleepwalking. I heard you."

Benny had no idea what Violet was talking about. "I didn't get up. But I think I heard somebody, too. Maybe it was Henry."

"It wasn't me," Henry said. "I slept like a rock last night."

"We better hurry up and get ready," Jessie said. "Mr. Bindry will arrive any minute to finish pricing the books. And the painters are coming today."

"Can we go down to the shop right now?" Benny asked. "Maybe somebody left footprints or fingerprints in the baby powder or dropped some of those pieces of paper we hid all over the place."

Henry said, "I've already checked the shop. If anybody was snooping there last night, they didn't walk on the floor or touch anything. The only prints down there now are the ones we made last night."

"Darn!" Benny said.

Henry had another idea. "Don't be too disappointed, we can try some other detective tricks. How would you like to shadow any suspicious people we see today?"

Benny liked this new idea very much. "Like they do in Miss Chase's books? Goody!"

Jessie laughed. "That's if we can find someone to follow, Benny. Now shadow me out to the kitchen for breakfast."

Jessie and Benny played a tracking game, but it didn't go very well. Benny tried to follow his sister down the long apartment hallway. But whenever Jessie turned around, Benny bumped smack into her!

"What are you children laughing about so early in the morning?" Miss Chase asked.

Jessie could hardly stop giggling. "Benny's trying to shadow me, but he keeps bumping into me instead."

"Well, shadows are attached to people, so that's why I stayed close to Jessie," Benny said. "Anyway, we're going to follow any suspicious people we see. Maybe one of them is the person who ran down the street last night!"

Miss Chase loved Benny's plan. "Well, let me give you a few tracking tips. First off, you don't want to stay so close to the person that you bump into them! Just tiptoe a few feet behind or nearby, not too close and not too far."

"What if the suspect sees me?" Benny wanted to know.

"You can pretend to be doing something else," Jessie said. "Tying your shoe or something like that."

Miss Chase looked very pleased. "You children seem to know my books inside out. I'm sure if anyone is up to something around the Aldens, he or she won't get away with it for long. You've learned all my little mystery tricks. Now all you need is a suspect."

"Speaking of suspects, Miss Chase," Jessie said, "we suspect someone was following us around yesterday when we went sightseeing. Let me get my backpack, and I'll show you what I'm talking about."

Jessie ran back to the sleeping porch. As

she was leaving, she saw someone in the courtyard. It was Mr. Bindry.

"Good morning, Mr. Bindry," Jessie cried out in her friendliest voice. "My brothers and sister and I will be right down in a minute to help you out."

She waved at Mr. Bindry, but he wasn't in a waving mood.

"He's always so crabby," Jessie said to herself as she walked back to the kitchen. "He even pretended not to see me!"

"So let's see what you children were up to in New Orleans yesterday," Miss Chase said when Jessie spread out her photos on the table. "Ah, what a nice shot of the Café du Monde! All that's missing are the *beignets*."

"That's because we ate them all," Benny said proudly.

Miss Chase picked up another photo. "I see you visited the cemetery."

"And you know what?" Violet asked in a quiet voice. "We saw a funeral procession. And a small band playing music. People waved to us to walk behind the band in the procession, too. Isn't that strange?"

"No," Miss Chase explained, "people down here find the music and the funeral processions a comfort to them when a person dies. It's okay for strangers to join them."

Miss Chase went through Jessie's photos one by one. Suddenly she was perfectly still.

"Is something the matter, Miss Chase?" Violet asked.

Miss Chase said, "I just noticed something strange about these pictures, that's all."

Benny could sit quiet no longer. "I know! I know! You saw Mr. Phillips, too! That's what we saw when we looked at all the pictures together."

"You children are even better detectives than I thought," Miss Chase said. "Wait just a second."

Miss Chase went out to the living room and pulled out something from her desk. When she came back to the kitchen table, she had a large magnifying glass in her hand. "Let's get a closer look."

"Now there's no mistaking that this is

Mr. Phillips," Henry said when he looked through the magnifying glass.

"The question is, why was Rex Phillips following you?" Miss Chase asked. "Did he come up to you at all, wave, or say anything?"

Jessie shook her head. "We were so busy having a good time, we didn't notice him at all until we looked at the pictures. The only person we ran into that we knew was Sarah."

"Sarah Deckle?" Miss Chase cried. "Where did you see her?"

"Near Jackson Square," Jessie explained. "It was kind of strange, too. I put down my backpack on a bench so I could read my map, and my backpack disappeared."

Henry broke in. "Then we saw Sarah Deckle walking up ahead with Jessie's backpack. She said she was on her way to the Lost and Found to turn it in."

"And you know what?" Benny asked. "She didn't even seem glad that Jessie turned up."

Miss Chase took off her glasses and seemed

to be thinking. Finally, she spoke up. "Was everything there when you got it back from Miss Deckle?"

"Yes," Jessie said. "Kleenex, a small Thermos, my camera, my wallet, and Violet's *Little Mermaid* book. She'd brought it along to read. . . ."

Suddenly Violet said, "I'm going to put *The Little Mermaid* back with the other books." Violet ran up to the sleeping porch.

She was back in a couple of minutes. "The rest of the fairy tales are missing!" Violet cried out.

"When was the last time you saw them?" Miss Chase asked the children.

"I don't remember," Jessie said.

"I'm not sure either," Violet added. "I gave Jessie *The Little Mermaid* to bring along when we went out yesterday. I put the rest of the set by my bed. But I can't remember when I last saw them on the night table."

"You mean they disappeared last night?" Henry asked.

Benny crinkled his forehead. "Or maybe

while we were having breakfast this morning."

Jessie thought of something else. She leaned over the balcony. "Mr. Bindry, Mr. Bindry," she called down.

"Why are you calling Mr. Bindry?" Benny asked.

"He was here just a few minutes ago," Jessie answered. "Maybe he saw someone come up the stairs to the sleeping porch."

"Or maybe," Henry said in a low voice, "Mr. Bindry was the someone who came up to the sleeping porch."

"Guess what?" Benny asked. "Now we have a suspect."

CHAPTER 8

The Aldens Set a Trap

Suspect or not, Mr. Bindry was still his grumpy old self when he reappeared an hour later.

"Can we help you carry those heavy books?" Henry asked.

"Hrmph," was Mr. Bindry's answer. "These are my price guides, and I can carry them myself."

"Did you have to go back home to get your guides after I saw you before?" Jessie asked.

"What business is that of yours, young

lady?" Mr. Bindry said sharply. "Now let me get on with my job."

Mr. Bindry went off to the far end of the courtyard as far as he could get from the Aldens.

"I'm going to follow Mr. Bindry so he doesn't get away again," Benny announced.

He headed into the bookshop and came out carrying a feather duster. Slowly he made his way across the courtyard, dusting the book tables high and low. Very soon he was where he wanted to be — right by Mr. Bindry.

"These books don't need dusting," Mr. Bindry told Benny.

Benny just kept right on with his feather dusting. He was going to track Mr. Bindry no matter what. If the man had Violet's books, Benny was going to do his best to find them.

A few minutes later, Violet came over, too. When Mr. Bindry saw Violet, he buried his nose in a book.

"How do you decide what to charge for a book?" Violet said to break the silence.

"Because I know what I'm doing!" Mr. Bindry muttered without looking up from his price guide.

"I've made some of my own books," Violet said shyly. "Would you like to see one of them?"

Mr. Bindry looked up over the top of his glasses. "If I take a look, will you and this boy let me work in peace? I trip over him every time I turn around."

"Sorry," Benny apologized, even though he hadn't come quite *that* close.

Violet reached into her tote bag. She pulled out a pretty fabric-covered book. "I made this scrapbook. Would you like to see it?"

Mr. Bindry pushed up his glasses to get a better look.

"Hmm," he said. He slowly turned the pages to see how she had mounted some of her photos and souvenirs. Mr. Bindry handed Violet back her book. "I've got to get to work, little girl. Now take your book away and your brother as well."

"I made a book, too," Benny announced.

"It's a flip book of a monkey climbing a banana tree." He reached into Violet's tote bag. "Want to see it?"

"The only books I have time for are Miss Chase's," Mr. Bindry barked at the children. "That's the job she hired me to do."

Benny and Violet looked at each other. It was time.

"How did you hear about this job?" Violet asked, a little nervous about what the answer might be.

Mr. Bindry ignored the question and didn't look up from his guide.

"The job," Violet repeated. "How did you hear about it?"

"There was an ad in the paper for anybody to see," Mr. Bindry said gruffly. "Now would you two run along and leave me be? I can't do what I was hired to do with kids running around touching everything."

Violet took Benny by the hand. "Making friends with Mr. Bindry isn't going to be easy," she said after they left the old man. "But it's the only way we'll ever find out anything. Mr. Bindry didn't lie exactly. He was right. The job was in the newspaper just as he said."

"But he showed up *before* it was in the paper," Benny said. "So it's kind of a lie."

"I know," Violet said quietly. "We'll just have to get to know Mr. Bindry better so we can find out why he isn't telling the truth."

"Did you have any luck with Mr. Bindry?" Jessie asked when Violet and Benny returned to the bookshop. "Miss Chase says she'll try to talk to him later while they're working together. She wants to know why he showed up for the job before it was in the paper."

"We tried, but he didn't say anything," Violet said.

"We'll just have to keep trying," Jessie said. "Meantime, this bookshop is still a regular dust bowl. I'm just sweeping up. Benny, can you grab that dustpan and help me out?"

While Jessie swept, Benny held out the dustpan. But working didn't keep him from talking a mile a minute. Today, nothing but Mr. Bindry and Violet's missing books were on his mind. "First he got his book guides, Jessie. Then he tried to go far away from us, but I didn't let him. I just kept dusting right near him the whole time. He wouldn't look at my monkey book, though."

Jessie smiled down at Benny. "Well, I *love* your monkey flip book. Did you and Violet get a chance to ask about the three missing fairy tales?"

"No way!" Benny said. "He didn't want us around. Violet said we should try to make friends little by little, then ask about her books."

"Not a bad idea, Benny," Jessie said as she swept near the brick wall of the bookshop. "I can't believe I have to sweep here again. These bricks keep crumbling all over no matter how much I dust and sweep."

"Hey," Benny said, taking a closer look at the wall. "Maybe there's a mouse hole, and that's why the pieces keep falling on the floor." Benny felt some of the bricks to see if they jiggled. "Hey, here's a loose one."

"Watch it, Benny!" Jessie said. But it was too late. Several loose chunks of brick tumbled down after Benny pulled out one of the bricks.

Benny didn't care one bit about the mess he was making. "I bet a mouse really does live in there," he said. He stood on tiptoe and tried to see inside the empty space. "Can I stick my hand in?"

"Be careful," Jessie warned.

Benny reached into the dark hole and felt around. "Somebody just stuffed paper and rags in here to keep out the cold." He pulled out some bunched-up yellow newspapers and rags. Then he tossed the papers into a can Henry was getting ready to put at the curb for recycling.

The Aldens went back to work. Soon the bookshop was clean.

"A couple of coats of paint, some new books, and the Mystery Bookstore will be ready for business," Henry said. "I'll take this can out to the sidewalk for pickup."

Just as Henry got to the front door of the shop, it opened.

"Is Miss Chase here?" Rex Phillips asked Henry. "I need to talk to her right away."

"She had to meet with somebody about

ordering books for her bookstore," Jessie answered. "Can we help?"

"I doubt it." Mr. Phillips shifted from one foot to the other. "Look, you kids tell her I'm going to offer her a good price for all those books out in the courtyard. She can cancel the sale tomorrow. Have her call me right away."

"We'll give her the message," Henry said. "But I don't think she'll cancel the sale after all this work. Everybody's looking forward to it."

"Not everybody," Mr. Phillips said under his breath. He reached for the door, but Benny was in the way.

"I need to get by," Mr. Phillips said. But when he moved sideways, Benny moved sideways too. He kept right on sweeping invisible dirt into the dustpan as if he didn't even see Mr. Phillips!

Benny had Mr. Phillips trapped between the counter and the door. Right away, Jessie figured out what to do. She took Violet's scrapbook and spread out the children's sightseeing pictures. "Would you like to take a look at our photos of New Orleans?"

Mr. Phillips's face almost turned purple. "I'm a businessman. I haven't got time to look at a bunch of children's vacation pictures. Now would you move out of my way, little boy?"

"In a minute," Benny said, not budging at all. "There are a lot of dustballs down here."

"Dustballs!" Mr. Phillips yelled. "I haven't got time for dustballs, either."

"Did you know you were in our pictures?" Violet asked. "Look. Here you are behind me and Benny in the café, then down at the docks, and a few other places, too. That's you, isn't it?"

"Nonsense," Mr. Phillips said. "I was in Lafayette yesterday at a stamp show." With that, Mr. Phillips practically jumped over Benny and stormed out.

"He didn't like our pictures too much," Henry said.

Jessie gathered up her photos. "Maybe he was at a stamp show yesterday, but he was also in Jackson Square and at the docks and

lots of other places right here in New Orleans. I'm sure of that."

"I have to go out to put this recycling can
at the curb," Henry said. "I'll follow Mr.
Phillips for a while the way we planned."

The other Aldens went over to the bookshop window to watch Henry watch Mr.
Phillips.

"Hey!" Benny cried. "Why is Henry reading one of those old newspapers instead of
staying behind Mr. Phillips?"

"Let's find out," Jessie said.

Henry seemed to have forgotten all about
Mr. Phillips. Instead he was reading an old,
wrinkled newspaper that was practically falling apart.

"Why aren't you shadowing Mr. Phillips?"
Benny asked.

Henry handed Jessie the newspaper.
"Never mind Mr. Phillips right now. Just
take a look at this. It's one of those old newspapers you pulled out from behind that brick
wall, Benny. It caught my eye when I put
down the can. Read what it says under this
picture."

The Aldens squinted at a faded picture of a smiling, middle-aged woman. She was holding open a little album of some kind with a small rectangular stamp in the middle. Jessie began to read:

"Local resident, Mabel Post, holds up a rare Costa Rican stamp showing a reversed flag. Mrs. Post, owner of the Old Treasures Bookshop, found the album in a one-dollar box of children's books she bought at a local yard sale. She would not discuss what she planned to do with the valuable stamp."

Benny was puzzled. "What does that mean? How come if a stamp is reversed it's worth more than one that's the right way?"

Henry, who knew a little about stamp collecting, had heard about the famous backwards flag stamp. "Because when the post office found the mistake, it stopped printing the wrong ones. I think they only printed a sheet of a hundred stamps of the backwards flag, so each stamp is worth a lot."

"I wonder what happened to this one," Violet said. "Miss Chase said Mrs. Post could hardly keep her shop going. Wouldn't she have been rich if she had sold the stamp?"

CHAPTER 9

Some Very Old News

That afternoon, Benny looked for Miss Chase from the parlor window. Finally, very late in the day, she came around the corner. Benny flew downstairs, through the courtyard, and out to the street.

"Goodness, I didn't know we were expecting Hurricane Benny," Miss Chase said with a laugh. "What's up? Watching the bookshop get painted can't be that exciting!"

"This is what's exciting!" Benny handed Miss Chase the old newspaper with Mabel Post's picture.

"Phew, you're going awfully fast for me, Benny," Miss Chase said. "Let's go upstairs so I can get my reading glasses. Then I can see what you have here."

"It's . . . it's about Mrs. Post buying a stamp with a flag that's the wrong way. And Henry said wrong-way stamps are worth lots more than right-way ones."

"I haven't a clue what you're talking about," Miss Chase said. "And Rex Phillips has been bothering me all day. He tracked me down to the office where I was meeting with some book people and waited for me until I came out. I only got rid of him by telling him that we have our book sale tomorrow, rain or shine."

"Oops, I almost forgot," Benny said. "He told us to tell you he wanted to buy all the books all by himself and not have the book sale. But Henry said no way. And know what else?"

Miss Chase laughed again. "No, what?"

"He said he wasn't in our pictures and that he went to a stamp show."

By this time, Benny and Miss Chase were

back in the apartment with the other Aldens.

Miss Chase rummaged in her purse for her reading glasses. Then she took a good long look at the old newspaper Benny handed her and read the headline: "FLOODWATERS DAMAGE HISTORIC FRENCH QUARTER."

"No, not that side." Jessie flipped over the page so Miss Chase could see Mabel Post's picture. "This side."

"My goodness, doesn't Mabel look young here?" Miss Chase said. "This is way before I moved to New Orleans, of course. Ah yes, I'd heard these stories about her buying a valuable stamp in a box of old books at a yard sale. But Mabel never admitted to it, and I never bothered to track down the story. Now I see why people didn't really remember the facts too well."

"Why's that, Miss Chase?" Henry asked.

Miss Chase flipped over the newspaper page. "Mabel's picture appeared on the same day as a terrible flood here in New Orleans. We get many of them during hurricane season. The day Mrs. Post's picture was in the

paper was one of the worst floods ever. No wonder people don't remember about the stamp."

"Did Mrs. Post ever mention the backwards flag stamp to you?" Jessie asked.

Miss Chase thought a bit. "Not really. Sometimes when Rex came around, she'd joke about having lots of valuable stamps hidden away. But she always wound up telling Rex that stamp collecting was just child's play or that stories about her having a valuable stamp were nothing but fairy tales. Of course, this upset Rex to no end. Pretty soon he'd try to get something out of her. But as far as I know, he never had a bit of luck."

"Speaking of luck, we didn't have any luck finding the missing books," Violet said.

"It's just the oddest thing the way those books just disappeared off the sleeping porch," Jessie said. "I bet Mr. Bindry had something to do with it. He *was* in the courtyard this morning."

"And after that he shooed me and Violet away," Benny complained. "Anyhow, at least I found this boring old newspaper in the mouse hole."

Miss Chase patted Benny's hand. "Now, Benny, a good detective like you knows that a clue doesn't have to look exciting to be exciting."

This got Benny thinking. He picked up the old newspaper and went over to the mirror with it. Holding it up, he said: "Now the stamp doesn't look backwards. It looks like a regular old stamp now. But everything else in the picture looks backwards." Then he put the newspaper on the table and ran over to Miss Chase's desk. "Can I borrow the magnifying glass?"

"Sure," Miss Chase answered. "Do you want a better look at the stamp?"

"Not the stamp!" Benny cried. He slid the newspaper under the light over the kitchen table.

"What do you see?" Violet asked when she looked over Benny's shoulder. "Omigosh! Look what else is in the picture! Mrs. Post is holding the boxed set of fairy tales on her lap with one hand and the stamp album with the other!"

Now everyone crowded around to see what Benny and Violet were hollering about.

"You're quite right, children," Miss Chase said when she got a good look at the photo, too. "Mabel Post has her other hand resting right on *The Little Mermaid*."

CHAPTER 10

Benny and Violet Hide Out

By seven o'clock on Saturday morning, the sun was up. It was a perfect day for an outdoor book sale. In just a couple hours, the Mystery Bookstore would be ready for its first customers.

"It's almost your last day in New Orleans, so I don't want to work you children too hard," Miss Chase said as she enjoyed a cup of her favorite chicory coffee. "You've all done so much already. Now that your grandfather is back, he's offered to take over some of the work so you children can do some last-minute sightseeing."

Mr. Alden put down his coffee cup. "If I know my grandchildren, I have a feeling they'd rather be at the bookstore sale than go sightseeing, Olivia."

"That's right, Grandfather," Benny agreed. "We're going sightseeing right here. Today's the day we find the rest of Violet's set and maybe that funny backwards stamp, too."

Mr. Alden laughed. "You'd better bring me up to date on all your plans, Benny."

"Violet and I thought up everything last night," Benny said. "We're going to hide under the children's book table and listen to who snoops around too much."

"I see," Mr. Alden said. "And who might be snooping about?"

Benny took a deep breath. "Well, first there's Mr. Bindry. He came for the job before it was in the newspaper."

"Don't forget Sarah Deckle," Henry reminded everyone. "She always shows up at odd times."

"Her, too," Benny said. "And Mr. Phillips 'cause he likes stamps, and the backwards stamp is missing. If anybody else gets too snoopy, we're going to watch them, too."

"You're going to be very busy," Mr. Alden remarked.

"And know what else?" Benny asked. "We tied one end of a spool of thread to *The Little Mermaid*. You can hardly see it. If anybody tries to take it away, we'll be able to tell."

"Just don't sell it by mistake," Miss Chase reminded the children.

"Oh, we won't," Violet said.

"It's almost nine o'clock," Miss Chase said. "Now I want you children to have some fun today and not work too hard. Promise?"

"Promise," Jessie said. "But work is fun for us."

Working at the book sale *was* fun for the Aldens, just as Jessie said. Since they loved reading mysteries — and solving them — Jessie and Henry decided to work at the mystery table.

"People sure get up early when there's a

BOOK
SALE
TODAY

sale," Henry said, after he let the first customers into the courtyard. "We're going to be very busy."

"So are we," Violet giggled from under the children's book table nearby. "All I can see are feet, Benny. Jessie said she'd tap on the top of the table if one of our suspects comes in."

Violet and Benny didn't have to wait long.

"One tap!" Benny whispered to Violet when they heard Jessie rap the table once. "That means Mr. Bindry is coming over. Do you have the spool end of the thread?"

"I'm holding it." Violet tugged the thread gently from under the table.

"Good morning, Mr. Bindry," the younger children overheard Jessie say only a couple feet away. "Can I help you with anything this morning?"

"Hrmph," Mr. Bindry said before moving over to the children's table.

Violet and Benny could hardly sit still when they saw Mr. Bindry's shoes just inches from where they were hiding. Violet held tight to the thread.

Then the children heard another pair of feet march over to the children's table. Jessie tapped the table twice.

"It's Sarah Deckle," Benny whispered.

Violet felt a tug on the thread.

"What are you doing with that book, Miss?" Mr. Bindry asked. "I was about to buy it."

"Well, I picked it up first," Sarah Deckle answered.

Benny and Violet heard more footsteps. Then they saw a familiar pair of white and black sneakers.

"It's Henry," Benny whispered.

"Sorry, folks," Henry said. "This book isn't for sale. It belongs to my sister. The rest of the set is missing, and we're hoping someone will come by who knows about the set it belongs to."

Violet and Benny saw Sarah Deckle kick her toe at the ground. "Well, maybe your sister would like to sell it. I'll pay a hundred dollars just for this book."

Before Henry could answer, Mr. Bindry

had some angry words for Miss Deckle. "A hundred dollars? What do you know about books, anyway? This volume may be part of a limited edition set illustrated by Arthur Plumbrush, a famous painter. They were the only books he ever illustrated. The first printing completely sold out long ago, and the original art was destroyed in a fire. So the books could never be reprinted. A complete set would be nearly priceless."

"But Mr. Bindry, you told Violet her book wasn't worth much," Henry said. "Don't you remember?"

"What I remember is saying children and old books don't mix," Mr. Bindry snapped. "I'm going to check with Olivia to see why this book is just lying around in the first place."

Sarah Deckle looked as upset as Mr. Bindry. "Yes, do that," she said. "I'll be right here until you get back."

After Mr. Bindry left with Henry, the book sale got crowded. Benny and Violet could see many pairs of feet surrounding the book tables. Sarah Deckle's feet, though, never moved.

A few minutes later the younger children heard a familiar voice talking to Jessie. "Hello, young lady. I came by to buy a signed copy of *The Streetcar Mystery*," Mr. Phillips said to Jessie. "But I see there are none left. Can you check if Miss Chase has any more copies inside the shop?"

"Uh, maybe," Jessie said, "but I really can't leave until my brother Henry returns. He'll be back any second."

"I'll wait here," Mr. Phillips said. "You see, I'm in a bit of a rush today, and I'd like to get the signed copy. If you could just get Miss Chase to sign a book, I can be on my way."

"Well, okay," Jessie agreed. "Oops, I have to tie my shoe."

When Jessie bent down, she whispered to Benny and Violet: "I have to run into the shop for another book. Just make sure to hold onto that thread. Now Mr. Phillips *and* Sarah Deckle are here. I'll be right back."

As soon as Jessie was gone, Benny and

Violet heard Rex Phillips talking in a low voice to Sarah Deckle. This time he didn't sound so polite. "Drop the book into my briefcase. Quick, before those two nosy kids get back. Did you find the rest of the set in the apartment this morning?"

"No," Sarah Deckle whispered. "But if we're lucky, maybe the stamp is in this one. We can look for the rest of the set later when all these kids are busy working. Open your briefcase slowly, and I'll slip the book in."

Violet and Benny could hardly sit still in their hideout. Miss Deckle and Mr. Phillips were going to steal Violet's book together! The children felt the thread pull, so Violet let out the spool.

"Good," Mr. Phillips said in a low voice. "Now let's get out of here before anyone comes back and figures out the book is missing."

Violet broke the thread so Mr. Phillips wouldn't notice it was attached to the book. She grabbed Benny's hand. "Here's what we do. I'll sneak over to the courtyard door and close it so they can't get out that way. You go to the bookshop and tell Miss Chase what happened, okay?"

After Benny ran off, Violet didn't have to wait long for her two suspects.

"Excuse me, we have to leave." Mr. Phillips tried to get by Violet. "Just open the door."

"I'm sorry, I can't do that," Violet said. "Everybody has to go out through the bookshop."

Sarah Deckle's face got red. "Rex! You've got a key. Open up."

Rex reached into his pocket and pulled out the same key chain Violet had seen him drop a few days earlier. "Move out of the way," he said to Violet.

Violet didn't move.

Sarah Deckle looked panicked. "All right. Let's just get out through the bookstore."

Rex Phillips didn't need to be coaxed. He and Sarah elbowed their way through the crowd of customers until they were in the bookstore.

"It's too late," Sarah Deckle said when she

saw the Aldens, Mr. Bindry, and Miss Chase blocking their way.

"Stop right there, Rex!" Miss Chase said. "I need to check your briefcase before you leave. We have reason to suspect you've taken a book." She pointed to a sign above the cash register that said: "We reserve the right to inspect belongings. Shoplifters will be prosecuted to the full extent of the law."

Mr. Phillips had no choice. There seemed to be Aldens everywhere he looked. Finally, he handed over his briefcase to Olivia Chase.

Miss Chase opened it. *The Little Mermaid* was resting right on top of the old newspaper.

"Oh, my," Mr. Bindry gasped, "it really is the last book in the Plumbrush set. May I examine it, Olivia?"

Miss Chase stepped between Mr. Bindry and the book. "What do you know about the rest of the set, Ezra? Tell me right now."

Mr. Bindry seemed dizzy and confused. He leaned against the counter to steady himself. "The other three books are in the trunk of my car. Here, take my keys and get them, young man," Mr. Bindry said to Henry.

Henry was back in a minute with Violet's set.

"Here, young lady," Mr. Bindry said, handing all the books to Violet. "The set is rightfully yours. I know you'll treasure it because you're a book lover, too."

Violet's hands were shaking when she took the books from Mr. Bindry. "How did you get the other three?"

"I took them last night while all of you were out. I'm sorry. I still had a set of keys Mabel gave me. Please understand. I just *had* to see those books once Violet said *The Little Mermaid* was part of a set. I don't know how I missed them in Mabel's shop during my many visits."

"I found them mixed in with the hobby books, Mr. Bindry," Violet explained.

Now it was Mr. Phillips' turn to speak. "That's just another one of Mabel's cruel jokes on me! She was always teasing me about having valuable stamps and making me hunt down clues. I'd heard stories that she even had the famous Costa Rican flag stamp. I'm more of a stamp expert than any of the writers of those worthless hobby books, so I never bothered to check that section."

"What made you think the stamp might be connected with the fairy tales, Rex?" Miss Chase asked.

Mr. Phillips's eyes looked hard and angry. "It kept driving me crazy when she said stamp collecting was child's play or that those old stories about the famous stamp were just fairy tales."

"Where do you come in, Sarah?" Miss Chase wanted to know.

"Miss Post bought the flag stamp at my grandfather's for one dollar! One dollar!" Sarah Deckle began. "My poor grandfather didn't even know he had such a valuable stamp lying around. After he died, it was just thrown in with these old books and sold off in a yard sale! When I found an old newspaper in some family papers showing Miss Post with the stamp, well, I just had to get it back. I found out Rex knew all about stamps, so I showed him the newspaper."

"That's how I narrowed my search down to these books," Rex explained. "We followed the Aldens all week. Sarah nearly got hold of one of the books at Jackson Square, but it looks like Mr. Bindry beat us to the rest of the set."

"I'm sorry, Olivia," Mr. Bindry apologized. "I just had to see if you really had the entire Plumbrush set. I was hiding under the stairs in the courtyard early in the week when you told the Aldens you were going to advertise for a book expert. Only I showed up too soon, as these smart children figured out. Then Henry here caught me poking around when I thought you were all out to lunch the other day."

"Were you the person we saw run from the shop? We also had the feeling someone was looking around while we were sleeping," Henry said.

Mr. Bindry nodded his head. "I did come up the stairs while you were out to dinner. That's when I took the three books. But bother sleeping children? Never!"

"That was me," Sarah Deckle confessed

"I didn't mean to scare anyone. I just waited until everyone was asleep after you got back from sightseeing. Rex also had a set of Miss Post's keys. I let myself into the courtyard and came up to the sleeping porch. But, of course, the three books were already gone. I knew one of them was in Jessie's pack, but I didn't dare look for it at night. I came back in the morning, but the set was still gone. And I couldn't find Jessie's backpack."

"Never mind who did what with these books," Rex Phillips said. "What I want to know is, where is the flag stamp?"

Mr. Bindry picked up *The Little Mermaid*. He stroked the book gently then opened to the back of the book. He ran his fingers over the endpapers. No one dared to breathe. Mr. Bindry reached into his pocket and pulled out a small knife with a razor-thin blade. He put the blade under the endpaper and slowly lifted it away from the cover.

"The glue is all dried out," he said. "It's going to come right up."

And so it did. When Mr. Bindry lifted the endpaper, everyone gasped.

"There's the stamp!" Rex Phillips said, barely whispering. "Don't touch it. It's extremely fragile. What are you doing with that book, for heaven's sake?"

Mr. Bindry handed the book, stamp and all, to Violet. "It's rightfully yours, young lady. Take good care of it."

Violet took the book from Mr. Bindry and offered it to Miss Chase. "I want to give it back to you. You can sell the stamp and the books and buy your shop right now. Please take it back."

Miss Chase put her arm around Violet. "I should report Rex and Miss Deckle to the police. But they'll be more useful by helping me find out how we can sell this beautiful stamp. I may even share the money with Sarah Deckle to settle things with her family. But I want you to keep the fairy tales, Violet — the whole set."

Violet smiled. "Only if you'll display them at the Mystery Bookstore. That way I can see the books whenever we come to New Orleans."

Miss Chase turned to Mr. Bindry. "Ezra,

I know you've returned the books, but I can't help feeling terribly let down. After all, you and I have known each other for years. I don't see how we can work together now, I really don't."

Mr. Bindry looked crushed. "I don't blame you, Olivia. I put my own interest ahead of everyone. Please accept my deepest apology. I wish you would give me a chance to make it up to you."

Miss Chase stared at Mr. Bindry for a very long time. "How could you do that, Ezra, after all that's happened?"

"I could put together a rare book collection of mysteries for your store, that's what you could let me do, Olivia," Mr. Bindry suggested. "I don't read most of the books I collect, but I do know I have quite a valuable collection of rare mysteries myself. I'd like to give them to you for sale in your Mystery Bookstore. May I do that, Olivia?"

Miss Chase took a while to answer, but when she did, she was smiling. "Of course, Ezra. I know your collection would draw many mystery lovers to my new shop. Perhaps you and I can try to start over after all."

"Hey! What about a mystery from *my* collection?" Benny piped up.

"Now what mystery is that, young fellow?" Mr. Bindry asked.

Benny crinkled his forehead. "Well, it's not even written yet, but it will be. It's going to be about two brothers and two sisters who hear about a missing backwards stamp hidden in some old books. But the books get stolen and everything, and the kids have to find them. What do you think?"

Everyone laughed, including Mr. Bindry. "Now that's one mystery I'll actually have to read."

GERTRUDE CHANDLER WARNER discovered when she was teaching that many readers who like an exciting story could find no books that were both easy and fun to read. She decided to try to meet this need, and her first book, *The Boxcar Children*, quickly proved she had succeeded.

Miss Warner drew on her own experiences to write the mystery. As a child she spent hours watching trains go by on the tracks opposite her family home. She often dreamed about what it would be like to set up housekeeping in a caboose or freight car — the situation the Alden children find themselves in.

When Miss Warner received requests for more adventures involving Henry, Jessie, Violet, and Benny Alden, she began additional stories. In each, she chose a special setting and introduced unusual or eccentric characters who liked the unpredictable.

While the mystery element is central to each of Miss Warner's books, she never thought of them as strictly juvenile mysteries. She liked to stress the Aldens' independence and resourcefulness and their solid New England devotion to using up and making do. The Aldens go about most of their adventures with as little adult supervision as possible — something else that delights young readers.

Miss Warner lived in Putnam, Connecticut, until her death in 1979. During her lifetime, she received hundreds of letters from girls and boys telling her how much they liked her books.